Katie Woo

Star of the Show

by Fran Manushkin

illustrated by Tammie Lyon

PICTURE WINDOW BOOKS
a capstone imprint

Katie Woo is published by Picture Window Books,
151 Good Counsel Drive, P.O. Box 669
Mankato, Minnesota 56002
www.capstonepub.com

Library of Congress Cataloging-in-Publication Data
Manushkin, Fran.
Star of the show / by Fran Manushkin; illustrated by Tammie Lyon.
p. cm. — (Katie Woo)
ISBN 978-1-4048-6515-0 (library binding)
ISBN 978-1-4048-6613-3 (paperback)
[1. Theater—Fiction. 2. Chinese Americans—Fiction.] I. Lyon, Tammie, ill. II. Title.

PZ7.M3195Ssn 2011

[E]—dc22   2010030669

Summary: Katie's class puts on the play *The Princess and the Frog*.

Art Director: Kay Fraser
Graphic Designer: Emily Harris
Production Specialist: Michelle Biedscheid

Photo Credits
Fran Manushkin, pg. 26
Tammie Lyon, pg. 26

Printed in the United States of America in Stevens Point, Wisconsin.
042011
006196R

Table of Contents

Chapter 1
Casting Call 5

Chapter 2
Katie Practices..............................9

Chapter 3
Showtime!....................................13

Casting Call

Katie's class was putting on a play. "We're doing *The Princess and the Frog*," said Miss Winkle.

"Hooray!" said Katie.

"I want to be the princess!"

"Me too!" yelled JoJo.

"I want to be

the frog," said

Pedro. "I'm a

great hopper!"

"The parts are on these

cards," said Miss Winkle.

"Pick one to see which part

you get."

Katie picked
her card first.

"Oh, no!" she groaned.

"I'm not the princess. I'm a

worm!"

"I'm the princess!" yelled

JoJo.

"And I'm the frog!" said

Pedro.

"Good for you," said

Katie. But she felt sad. "A

worm cannot be a star,"

she sighed.

Chapter 2

Katie Practices

Katie told her dad, "It's no fun to be a worm. All I do is wiggle."

Her dad said, "You are crafty, Katie. You'll be a great worm."

Katie asked her mom,

"What does crafty mean?"

"It means clever," said her

mom. "I know you will be

the best worm you can be!"

Katie tried to be a great
worm. She worked hard on
her wiggling. She wiggled
forward, and she wiggled
backward.

Pedro and JoJo worked

hard on their parts, too.

JoJo told Pedro, "Don't

forget to kiss me so you can

turn into a prince."

Pedro nodded. "Sure,

sure."

Chapter 3

Showtime!

The big day came, and
the curtain went up.

"This is so exciting!" said
Katie.

"Oh, Frog," called the princess. "I threw my golden ball into the well. Will you get it for me?"

"Sure!" croaked the frog. He began hopping to the well.

"I can't see anything in

my costume," said Katie.

She wiggled close to Pedro

and almost tripped him!

"Oops," she thought.

"That was not crafty."

"Thank you for bringing me my golden ball," said the princess.

"Uh-oh," Katie whispered. "The tree is swaying! It's going to fall down!"

Katie wiggled over and
leaned on the tree.

"Stop that!" hissed the
tree. "I'm swaying in the
wind! I'm not falling down!"

It was time for
the frog to kiss the
princess, but the
frog didn't move.
He looked scared.

"Kiss her!" whispered Miss
Winkle.

The frog still did not move.

But Katie did!

She wiggled over and
whispered, "If you don't kiss
the princess, this worm will
kiss YOU!"

"EW!" said Pedro.

He kissed the princess.

"You are now a prince!"

she said.

The audience clapped and

cheered, "Hurray!"

As the princess took a

bow, her crown fell off —

and landed on the worm's

head!

Katie smiled and
wiggled. Everyone
clapped harder!
So Katie took a big
bow.

After the show, Pedro said,
"Katie, you were so clever!
You scared me into kissing
JoJo."

"Well," said Katie, "I
wanted you to be the best
frog you could be."

"And you were the craftiest worm," said Katie's dad.

"I guess a worm CAN be a star!" said Katie.

And everybody agreed.

About the Author

Fran Manushkin is the author of many popular picture books, including *How Mama Brought the Spring; Baby, Come Out!; Latkes and Applesauce: A Hanukkah Story;* and *The Tushy Book.* There is a real Katie Woo — she's Fran's great-niece — but she never gets in half the trouble of the Katie Woo in the books. Fran writes on her beloved Mac computer in New York City, without the help of her two naughty cats, Gilda and Goldy.

About the Illustrator

Tammie Lyon began her love for drawing at a young age while sitting at the kitchen table with her dad. She continued her love of art and eventually attended the Columbus College of Art and Design, where she earned a bachelors degree in fine art. After a brief career as a professional ballet dancer, she decided to devote herself full time to illustration. Today she lives with her husband, Lee, in Cincinnati, Ohio. Her dogs, Gus and Dudley, keep her company as she works in her studio.

Glossary

audience (AW-dee-uhnss)—the people who watch or listen to a performance

backward (BAK-wurd)—in the reverse direction

clever (KLEV-ur)—able to understand things or do things quickly and easily

crafty (KRAF-tee)—good at making things or figuring things out

curtain (KURT-uhn)—a piece of fabric pulled across a stage to cover it

hissed (HISSD)—said in a way that shows you do not like something or someone

sighed (SYED)—breathed out deeply to express sadness or relief

swaying (SWAY-ing)—moving from side to side

Discussion Questions

1. If you were in *The Princess and the Frog*, which part would you want, and why?

2. Do you think Miss Winkle's way of deciding parts for the class was fair? Are there other ways she could have decided?

3. Katie was disappointed about being a worm in the play. Have you ever felt disappointed? What happened?

Writing Prompts

1. What do you know about plays and the theater? Make a list of five words that have to do with plays or the theater.

2. Practice writing a description. Chose one of the costumes from the book, and write a sentence or two to describe how it looks.

3. Pretend you were at Katie's school play. Write a short review of the show. Be sure to say whether or not you liked it!

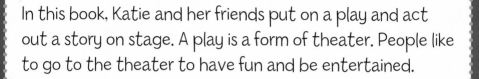

Having Fun with Katie Woo

In this book, Katie and her friends put on a play and act out a story on stage. A play is a form of theater. People like to go to the theater to have fun and be entertained.

Another type of theater is a puppet show. You can make your own puppets and make a show for your friends.

Finger Puppet Fun!

Make your own unique creatures or simple animals. It's up to you!

What you need:

- Pipe cleaners in several colors
- Small pom-poms in several colors
- Small googly eyes
- Craft glue
- Wire cutters or scissors

What you do:

1. Firmly wrap a pipe cleaner around your finger to form the body. As you near your finger tip, make the coils smaller until the finger tip is covered. Carefully slip your finger out.

2. Glue a pom-pom onto the top of the body. You may need to hold it there while it dries.

3. Now glue two googly eyes onto the pom-pom.

4. Finally, add arms, ears, beaks, or other details using pieces of pipe cleaners. Cut the pipe cleaner with a wire cutter or scissors. Fold the pieces into the shape you want. Then glue or twist them onto your puppet. Try making a cat with short pointy ears, a rabbit with long ears, or a bird with wings and a beak.

Make two or three puppets, then act out a story with them. Your friends and family will love to watch your puppet show!

THE FUN DOESN'T STOP HERE!

Discover more at www.capstonekids.com

- Videos & Contests
- Games & Puzzles
- Friends & Favorites
- Authors & Illustrators

Find cool websites and more books like this one at www.facthound.com. Just type in the Book ID: **9781404865150** and you're ready to go!